C.S.
Sto ✓

FRIEND ||||||||||||||||||||||||||||||||
OF ACPL   ◁ W9-BKU-250

j
Cosgrove, Stephen
Flutterby

j   1996384
    Cosgrove
    Flutterby

ALLEN COUNTY PUBLIC LIBRARY

FORT WAYNE, INDIANA 46802

You may return this book to any agency, branch,
or bookmobile of the Allen County Public Library

DEMCO

FLUTTERBY

written by: Stephen Cosgrove
illustrated by: Robin James

82 9059 2

Copyright 1976, Serendipity Communications, Ltd. All rights re-
served. No part of this book may be reproduced in any form without
permission from the publisher, except for brief passages included
in a review appearing in a newspaper or magazine.

Printed in the U.S.A.

ISBN#O-915396-12-2

P.O. Box 707
Bothell, Washington 98011

1996384

Dedicated to Denise Herrmann and Jerry Mills two people who are the spirit of Flutterby.

S. Cosgrove

In a burst of laughter and moonshine one fine and beautiful evening, Flutterby was born. As her silver-blue cocoon shimmered in the starlight she unfurled her wings and whinnied at the crystal night.

For, you see, Flutterby was not a common bug or butterfly but rather a smallest of small, winged, white flying horse.

She looked about and with a twinkle in her eye she set off to discover her new world. The dawn of a new morning warmed her wings as she soared just as high as she could fly.

She soared up and around for an hour or more as her wings grew stronger and stronger. Finally she thought, "I wonder what I am and what I'm to do?" She was thinking long and hard when suddenly Flutterby noticed a group of ants working industriously far below. "That's what I must be!" she exclaimed and with that she glided softly to the ground to join her own kind.

The ants ignored Flutterby as she landed amongst them but she watched with much interest as they busily dashed about gathering food and carrying it to their hill.

"Well!" she thought. "If I am truly an ant then maybe I should get to work too!"

She picked up some food, like the other ants, and carried it over to the hill.

She started to back down the ladder at the entrance to the ant hill when she realized that she didn't fit through the opening. In fact she got stuck halfway in and halfway out.

She began to whinny in absolute fear, but the patient ants, with some of them pushing from inside and the others pulling from the outside, yanked her from the ant hill.

Sobbingly Flutterby said, "If I'm an ant, then why don't I fit in our home?"

"Silly creature!" scolded one of the ants. "You're not one of us."

"But what am I then?" she asked.

"We don't know," they said. "Maybe you're a Honeybee." and with that they all went back to work, chuckling and shaking their heads.

"Maybe they're right," she said as a tear dropped from her eye. "Maybe I am a honeybee." So, Flutterby flew just as high as she could fly and suddenly below she saw a drove of honeybees collecting nectar from a patch of clover.

Quickly she folded her wings and like a hawk swept quickly to the ground. She watched them very closely to see exactly what they were doing. Then, following their every move, she carefully slipped into the blossom of a stock of clover and scooped up an arm load of nectar.

With her wings fluttering furiously she flew into line with the other honeybees who were heading for the hive.

When she arrived and it was her turn, she deposited the nectar where the other bees had placed theirs.

"That wasn't so bad," she thought. "I guess I really must be a bee!" Contented, she decided to explore her new home and everything would have been fine except that she backed into a bee. Now the bee never really meant to sting her but accidentally he did.

With a flick of her tail and a high-pitched whinny, Flutterby jumped straight into the air and landed right in the middle of a honeycomb.

The bees all started buzzing around laughing at the poor little horse as she sat stuck in the center of all that honey. "Silly creature!" they laughed "You're not a honeybee."

"But what am I?" she cried as a honey-coated tear dripped from her eye.

"We don't know," they said as they pulled her from the honeycomb "Maybe you're a butterfly." And with that they sent her on her way.

Flutterby sadly flew just as high as she could fly up where the sun is at its purest, and as she looked around for some butterflies the honey melted from her hooves and dropped like a golden rain.

From her high vantage point she sighted below hundreds of beautiful butterflies softly circling an old elm tree.

Hoping that these surely must be her people, she swooped down with a kick and a giggle to join her own kind.

She landed on the edge of a branch and watched her fellow butterflies floating gently on the breeze. "Ahh," she thought "I must surely be a butterfly." So, she spread her wings, stepped from the branch and tried to float on a whisper of the wind. She floated for just a moment but then began to fall. She flapped her wings furiously to gain some altitude and tried to float again but this time she fell down into the branches and onto a big flat leaf.

She just sat there and cried and cried. Finally a wise old Monarch butterfly flew up to her and asked, "Why are you crying?"

"I don't know what I am!" sobbed Flutterby. "When I came from my cocoon I flew just as high as I could fly and I spied the ants but they told me I wasn't an ant. So I flew just as high as I could fly and I spied the bees but they laughed at me and told me I wasn't a bee. Then, just now, I flew just as high as I could fly and I spied the butterflies. I tried to float like a butterfly but I couldn't so I can't be a butterfly. I just don't know what I am."

The old butterfly thought for a moment and then told Flutterby to look down through the leaves and to tell him what she saw.

Very carefully she leaned over the leaf and looked below. "I see a pool of water," she said.

"Now," said the butterfly," look closer and tell me what you see."

"I see a tiny horse with wings upon its back," said Flutterby. Then she became very excited, "Why that's me I see!" After looking at herself for a moment she asked, "But what am I?"

"You are you. Just as I am me," said the wise old butterfly. "Nothing more, nothing less."

"But what does a 'me' do?" she asked.

"Let's see," thought the butterfly. "You have very strong wings and can fly higher than high. You can whinny as loud as the wind and can see for miles. Hmm. I know what you should do. You should be the guardian sentry of fall for all the creatures of the forest. What you must do is fly as high as you can fly and watch for the approach of the winds of frost. When you see them, you must warn us, for all of the butterflies, the ants and all of the bees must hide from the winter, and the frost is the first warning."

Flutterby was so happy that she had found herself and something to do that she loved to do . . . flying just as high as she could fly.

So on some Autumn morning
Look into the frosty pool
You'll see in your reflection
That you're a Flutterby too!

BOOKS FROM SERENDIPITY

Written by Stephen Cosgrove

In Search of the Saveopotomas (1.25)

The Gnome From Nome (1.25)

The Muffin Muncher (1.25)

The Wheedle on the Needle (1.25)

Serendipity (1.25)

The Dream Tree (1.25)

Jake O' Shawnasey (1.25)

Hucklebug (1.25)

Morgan and Me (1.25)

Creole (1.25)

Flutterby (1.25)

Bangalee (1.25)

How to Plant a Bunch of Stuff (1.25)

How to Cook a Bunch of Stuff (1.25)

Boxed Set (5 Books) 6.00

Serendipity Coloring Book (1.00)

To order send cost of the books plus .25 postage and handling to:

Serendipity
P.O. Box 707
Bothell, Washington 98011

(Washington residents, please include sales tax of 5.4% with purchase.)